ARE *you* SITTING Comfortably?

FOR MAX, who I just KNOW is going to LOVE books

Bloomsbury Publishing, London, Oxford, New Delhi, New York and Sydney
First published in Great Britain in 2016 by Bloomsbury Publishing Plc
50 Bedford Square, London, WC1B 3DP

Text & illustrations copyright © Leigh Hodgkinson 2016
The moral right of the author/illustrator has been asserted

A CIP catalogue record of this book is available from the British Library

ISBN 978 1 4088 6482 1

Printed in China by C & C Offset Printing Co Ltd, Shenzhen, Guangdong

10 9 8 7 6 5 4 3 2 1
www.bloomsbury.com

All papers used by Bloomsbury Publishing are natural, recyclable products
made from wood grown in well-managed forests. The manufacturing processes
conform to the environmental regulations of the country of origin.

BLOOMSBURY is a registered trademark of Bloomsbury Publishing Plc

Merthyr Tydfil Public Libraries
Llyfrgelloedd Cyhoeddus Merthyr Tudful
Renew / adnewyddu:
Tel / *Ffon*: 01685 725258
Email / *Ebost*: library.services@merthyr.gov.uk
Catalogue / *Catalogau*: http://capitadiscovery.co.uk/merthyr/

Merthyr Tydfil
Leisure Trust
Ymddiriedolaeth Hamdden
Merthyr Tudful

Merthyr Tydfil Leisure Trust Limited - Company No 09192730 - Registered Charity No 1160014

ARE *you* SITTING Comfortably?

Leigh Hodgkinson

BLOOMSBURY

LONDON OXFORD NEW DELHI NEW YORK SYDNEY

The thing is . . .

when I want to read,

what I REALLY

REALLY need

is a place to sit . . .

just for a bit.

Somewhere comfy.

But NOT buzz-buzzy.

And NOT all

growly, itchy,

FUZZY.

Some place brighter.

WITHOUT these

HOOTS.

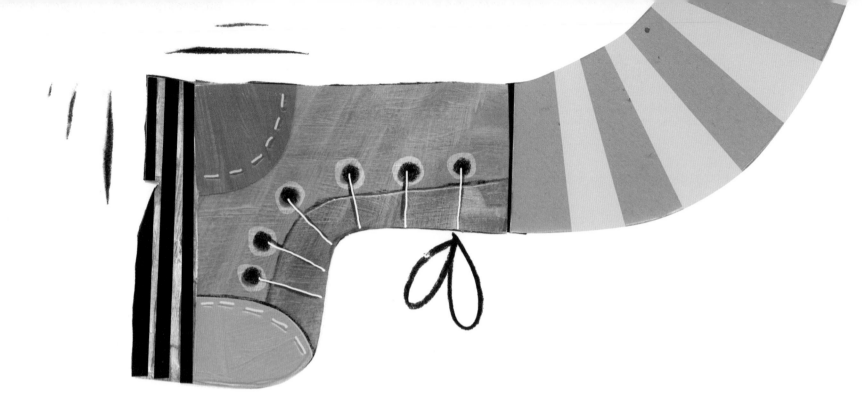

And 'NO!' to

GIANT

STOMPING boots.

A place NOT niffy,

StinKY

grimy.

Somewhere nice. NOT *slippy*, slimy.

(And I don't like soggy – sorry, Froggy!)

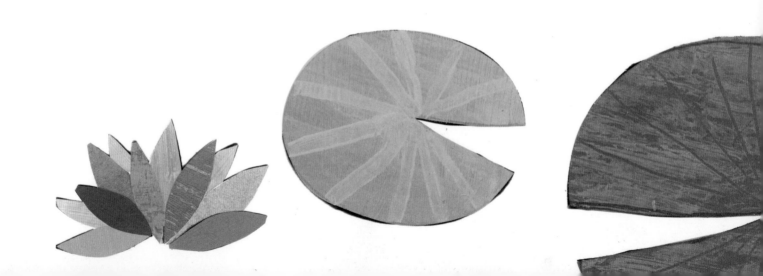

But it can't be far –

SORRY star!

It's GOT to be NOT hot, you see.

And NOT too

c o l d ...

. . . or up a TREE.

(This is WAY too high for me!)

Is this so very much to *ask?*

It seems to be a **MIGHTY** task.

But wait, hang on –

YES

THAT'S IT!

It doesn't matter

where you sit . . .

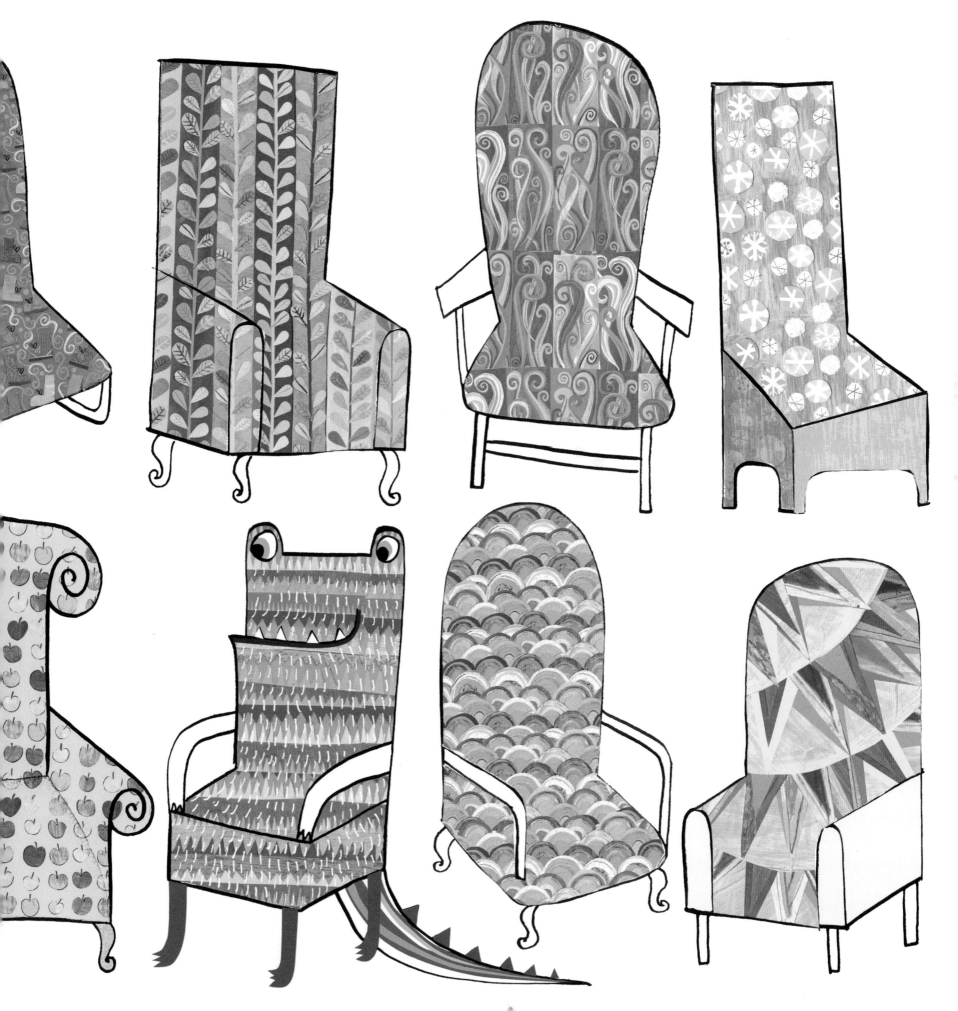

...a book is best **anywhere**...

a book is best when you SHARE.

And the boy, the cat,
the monster, the fox,
the butterfly,
the mouse, the frog,
the martian, the lion,
the polar bear
and the bird...
All read
happily
EVER AFTER.